Flaps, The Flying Squirrel

A Story of Caring for Others
& Believing in Yourself

By Karen Ravn

Illustrated by Cary Phillips

Hallmark

© 1999 HALLMARK CARDS, INC.
ISBN 0-87529-723-4

Benson Bear was the first one to see a crocus that spring. Lainie Lamb was the first to see a daffodil. And Fritz Frog was the first to see a tulip, though nobody ever knew because he was much too shy to tell.

But Miss Penelope Pig had the biggest "first" of all–she was the first one to see Flaps, the squirrel who claimed he could fly!

True, when Miss Penelope saw Flaps that first time, he was too sick to even think about flying. He was curled up under a tree in the forest, just lying there so small and still that Miss Penelope was afraid something was wrong. And something was! When she tried to wake him up, she couldn't. And when she felt his forehead, she could tell he had a very high fever.

"I better take him home with me," she told herself. When she picked him up, she saw a big F on his shirt. "Maybe that's his initial," she thought. "But who knows? I'll just call him Squirrel for now."

3

Miss Penelope carried Squirrel home and put him to bed in her guest room. Then she called her friends Lonnie and Bonnie Bunny, and they rushed right over. Bonnie, the town doctor, examined Squirrel and gave him some medicine. "Maybe that will help," she said.

But what if it didn't? Miss

Penelope couldn't bear to think about that. So she tried to look on the bright side–the way she always advised everyone else to do.

"I'll take super good care of Squirrel," she told the bunnies. "He can stay right here with me until he's all better."

Then Lonnie went out looking for anyone who knew anything about Squirrel.

Nobody did, but everybody came to visit him. When they saw how sick he was, they wanted to help Miss Penelope take care of him.

Mitzi Mouse helped by writing Miss Penelope's advice column for the newspaper—with Miss Penelope's advice, of course! "I just love writing," Mitzi said. "Don't you just love writing?"

Fritz Frog ran errands. "No problem," he said shyly. "It's fun to run."

Lainie Lamb whistled songs for Squirrel. "I sure hope he can hear," she said, "because whistling is sooooo hard."

Benson Bear tucked his favorite old teddy bear under Squirrel's blanket. "I'll miss that bear," Benson said. "But this little guy needs him now."

5

Bonnie kept checking on Squirrel, and Lonnie kept looking for clues about him, and their children, Lillie and Billy, drew him cheery pictures. "He'll see them when he gets better," Lillie said. "He is going to get better, isn't he, Miss Penelope?" she asked.

"I hope so," Miss Penelope said. "And I think so."

"But you don't know so?" Billy asked.

"Nobody can know so," Miss Penelope said, "not even me, but I think so—very, very much."

"Oh, good!" the bunnies said. "Then he will. You've never been wrong about anything, Miss Penelope!"

But Miss Penelope was afraid she might be wrong about this. Three whole days had gone by, and Squirrel didn't seem any better. So that night when she fluffed up his pillow and smoothed down his covers, Miss Penelope started to cry. "Oh, Squirrel," she said, "please get well. Please, please, please."

Miss Penelope spent the night in a chair by Squirrel's bed so she could hear if anything happened. And very early the next morning, when light was just barely starting to sneak in through the windows, something did happen. A very small, weak voice said, "Excuse me."

It was Squirrel—sitting up and looking very much better...and very much confused.

Miss Penelope jumped up and clapped her hooves and danced around the room. "You're better! You're better! You're better!" she sang.

Now Squirrel looked a little afraid. After all, he was a very small squirrel, and Miss Penelope was a rather large pig, and she was making a truly gigantic commotion! "Excuse me," he said again. "Who are you?"

Miss Penelope stopped still and calmed herself. "I'm Miss Penelope," she said gently.

"And I'm…I'm…" Squirrel started. Then he stopped. Then he started again. "I'm…I'm…" Then he stopped again.

Miss Penelope saw his lips quiver, and she heard his voice quaver, and she thought he might cry. "I don't know your name," she said quickly. "But I think it might start with an F."

Squirrel thought about that, and then his eyes lit up. "You're right!" he said happily. "I'm Flaps! I remember now!"

Miss Penelope had her doubts. She'd never heard of such a name! But still, it seemed like a good sign that Squirrel…er…Flaps…even thought he could remember something. "Hooray for you!" she said. "Do you remember anything else?"

Flaps just shook his head No three times. Miss Penelope saw a tear slide down his little cheek. "Don't worry," she said, gently patting his head. "It's just because you've been so sick. But you're feeling better now, and I'm here to take care of you. That's all that matters."

All the while Flaps had been sleeping, he hadn't eaten, and Miss Penelope was afraid he'd lost weight. Why, there were even little folds of loose skin hanging down under his arms. She fed him delicious meals and yummy snacks and made sure he ate every bite–with just a little help from her! But one day, Flaps said something amazing. "I'm eating as much as I can," he blurted out. "But I don't think I'll ever fill up all my loose skin. I think I need these flaps of mine." And he held his arms out wide so his loose skin didn't hang in folds anymore–it was stretched out into what he said…flaps!

"That does explain your name," Miss Penelope said. "But what do you need flaps for?"

"To fly," Flaps said.

That was too much for Miss Penelope. "Squirrels can't fly," she said. "It's a known fact."

"But flying is the one thing I can remember!" Flaps said.

Miss Penelope gave his little shoulder a little squeeze. "I'm afraid that's impossible," she said in her very kindest voice. "It's nothing to feel bad about though. I can't fly either! Neither can Mitzi nor Benson nor just about anybody else we know–not even Fritz, although he moves so fast it's almost like flying!"

Flaps never mentioned flying to Miss Penelope again, but he did mention it to Lillie and Billy and Lainie. They got very excited–until he told them that Miss Penelope didn't think he could do it.

"Oh," Lillie said. "Then you probably can't."

"Miss Penelope is never wrong," Billy said.

"She's sooooo smart," Lainie said.

So Flaps began to doubt himself. "Maybe I'm just imagining things," he thought. Still, sometimes when he was alone in the woods, he'd climb a tree and scamper out on a branch and spread his arms till his flaps were nice and tight, like wings–and he was almost sure he could take off and go swooping and gliding through the air! Almost sure. But not absolutely sure. After all, nobody else thought he could do it. So he'd always climb back down the tree again. "Maybe tomorrow," he'd tell himself.

Miss Penelope had worries of her own. Now that Flaps was well, he needed a permanent home. And she just wasn't sure he should stay with her.

"Why not?" Flaps asked when she told him.

"Oh, Flaps," she said, "I love having you here! But I've never been a mom before, and–don't tell anyone!–I don't know much about it–at least not as much as I know about everything else! So I'm just not sure that staying with me is the absolute best thing for you."

"You're not?" Flaps asked sadly.

Miss Penelope wanted to talk some more, but she saw Flaps' lips quiver, and she heard his voice quaver, and she thought he might cry. "We'll see," she said, and then she hugged him very tightly. As she did, a tear ran down her own cheek.

For days after that, Miss Penelope thought and thought and thought until she figured out what the absolute best thing really was. Then she invited everybody over so she could announce her pretty-much-perfect plan!

"We're having company today," she told Flaps on the morning of the meeting. "Let's decorate!" They filled all her vases with flowers, and they hung crepe paper streamers everywhere, and they put out the fancy tablecloth and punch bowl. Besides all of that, Miss Penelope made her chock-full-of-chocolate cake.

Naturally all their guests brought their own special goodies, too, so for a while, all anyone did was eat! Finally Miss Penelope called them to order. "As you know," she began, "Flaps has been staying with me temporarily, but now he needs a permanent home."

Flaps started to tremble. What if he had to leave Miss Penelope? He couldn't breathe because he was so scared of what she might say next.

"I've been thinking night and day about where that permanent home should be," she said next.

"He can live with us!" said the bunnies.

"Or with me!" said Mitzi.

"Or with me!" said everyone else, even Fritz, who had never, ever said anything in front of such a big group before.

They were all being nice, but they were ruining Miss Penelope's plan. So she thanked them very much–and then she went on with her speech. "As I was saying, I did a lot of thinking about where Flaps should live, and the more I thought, the surer I got–Flaps has to live with me, because the two of us…well…we're like a little family already, and I'm…well…I'm getting to feel like a mom!"

Finally Flaps started breathing again and smiling and smiling and smiling!

"At first I wasn't sure I could raise Flaps all by myself," Miss Penelope said. "But then I realized I don't have to! He has Lillie and Billy to play with and Benson and Mitzi to baby-sit..."

"He'll just love my baby-sitting," Mitzi said.

"...and he has Lainie to teach him to whistle..." Miss Penelope went on.

"Whistling is sooooo hard," Lainie said.

"...and Fritz to run races with him..." Miss Penelope continued.

"No problem," Fritz said.

"...because even though Flaps will live with me..."

"We can all be his family!" the bunnies said.

"Exactly!" Miss Penelope said. "We can all be his family!"

"Hooray!" everybody said. "We can all be his family!"

That's when Flaps started dancing around the room and hugging everybody, over and over. Then suddenly he knew exactly what he wanted to do–and he was absolutely sure he could do it! He grabbed a roll of crepe paper and ran outside. "Come watch!" he called. "I have a surprise!"

Everyone hurried outside after him. "There he is!" Lainie called, pointing up at a tall tree. And there he was–on a high branch, with his arms spread wide and his flaps pulled nice and tight, like wings–ready to take off!

"No, don't!" Miss Penelope cried. "Squirrels can't fly! It's a known fact!"

"And Miss Penelope is never wrong!" Lillie and Billy cried. "That's a known fact, too!"

But Flaps smiled proudly. "Don't worry," he called down to them. "I can do it!" And suddenly, he was doing it. He was flying–from branch to branch, up and down, back and forth–as if he'd been doing it all his life. For, in truth, some squirrels can fly, and Flaps was one of them!

"Of course, there's an exception to every rule," Miss Penelope said softly. Then she just watched in amazement, for Flaps wasn't only flying–he was spelling something out with the crepe paper. And soon everyone could read his special message to his brand-new, great big, happy family!

THE END

Flying Squirrels

There really are squirrels known as flying squirrels. But it is a funny name for them, since they don't really fly like birds or insects. Instead, they glide. They have a thin web of skin between their front and back feet. By spreading their legs, the squirrels pull this skin tight so that it works a little like a wing and a little like a parachute. They glide across short distances, and the place where they start has to be higher than the place where they land. There could be flying squirrels living near you. If you've never seen one, it might be because, unlike Flaps, they only come out at night.